Dragon Charmer

For Sear,
A future Dragon
Charmer, I'm sure.
I hope you like the story.

Godspeed
Ruth Siburt

by
Ruth Siburt

Royal Fireworks Press
Unionville, New York
Toronto, Ontario

For Matthew who wasn't satisfied with a short story.

Special thanks to Mike for understanding
and to Nan Rickelman for reading.

Royal Fireworks Press   Royal Fireworks Press
First Avenue   78 Biddeford Avenue
Unionville, NY 10988   Downsview, Ontario
(914) 726-4444   M3H 1K4 Canada
FAX: (914) 726-3824   FAX: (416) 633-3010

ISBN: 0-88092-350-4 Paperback
        0-88092-351-2 Library Binding

Printed in the United States of America using vegetable-based inks
on acid-free recycled paper by the Royal Fireworks Printing Co.
of Unionville, New York.

1

Dragon Song

She looked like an ordinary librarian—tall and thin with rimless glasses and wisps of silver-white hair escaping from the bun at the back of her head.

So I asked politely, "Please, Ma'am, can you tell me if you have any *new* vox-books on dragons?"

I had only half an hour to find all of the books on dragons I could to bring home with me.

Since my father died the December before, I had become Mother's "right arm girl." I was named for Elizabeth Cady Stanton: the strongest nineteenth century woman Father had ever read about. I was trying to be as strong as Mrs. Stanton, but it wasn't easy.

It seemed the only time I wasn't worrying about my mother or my four-year-old sister, Sara, or myself, was when I was reading or dreaming about dragons. And the only opportunity I had to gather dragon material was once a week while Sara attended library story time.

The woman peered at me through ancient eyes. "What do you know of dragons?"

"Everything. I've heard all of the dragon books here. These are my favorites." I tipped my stack of vox-books title out for her to touch.

"*Here Be Dragons, A Book of Dragons, St. George and the Dragon, The Legend of King Arthur.*" The titles read themselves aloud in a pleasant neutral voice.

1

The woman drew her hand away from the last book. "*King Arthur,* humph. He was a fine one. Nearly robbed the world of dragons—he and his knights."

She jabbed a strand of silvery hair back into the bun on her neck. Immediately, another sprang loose.

"If people knew how long it takes to grow dragons, or how much care they need. If they knew how rare and beautiful dragons are, and how they must struggle to survive, I doubt they would sing the dragon killers' praises quite so loudly." The woman took off her glasses and pointed the earpiece at me. "We'd see then who shouted 'Hurrah, Hurrah,' when a cruel knight plunged his sword into a dragon's breast."

"I would never shout hurrah," I said.

"You wouldn't?" The woman perched her glasses back on the bridge of her nose.

"No, I love dragons. They are fierce and brave and beautiful. I'd give anything to live in the time of knights and dragons. Not to kill the dragons, just to see them. To watch one blaze across the sky. To hear a dragon's song."

I clamped a hand over my mouth. I'd said too much.

"Dragon's song? How do you know about the dragon's song?" The woman leaned closer to me. "You didn't hear about *that* in your books."

"No, Ma'am."

I wondered if it was safe to tell her. I had never told anyone how much I knew of dragons that did not come from books but from the sort of waking dreams I dreamt almost every day.

I wanted to tell. It would be such a relief not to feel so odd and alone. But the woman was a grown-up.

Wouldn't she think I was making it up? Yes, and then she would laugh.

"Please, Ma'am, if you could tell me where there are any other vox-books, I'll...."

"Have you *heard* a dragon's song?"

"Well...." I had, of course, in my dreams. How else could I have known?

Their song was like a wind sighing high in the trees. It brushed against my skin like velvet rainbows and smelled of poppies. It piped notes the purest angels could not sing and the keenest ears could not hear.

The woman wrapped her arms around herself, cocking her head like a listening bird.

Watching the woman, I heard a single note from a dragon's song. Goose bumps prickled my arms. Here, in the middle of the library, on an ordinary Thursday, at four o'clock in the afternoon, I'd heard the song.

I glanced around at the children seated at low tables on brightly colored chairs, listening to books and working puzzles. But they seemed not to have heard. Or, if they had heard, they had not believed.

"Have you," I asked the woman, "heard the dragon's song?"

"Oh, yes," said the woman, "I was thirteen the first time. About as old as you, I'd judge."

I nodded.

"The song was so sweet, I never wanted to live without its sound echoing inside my chest. My poor mother thought I'd gone a little crazy." The woman drew a circle with her finger at her temple. "Small wonder, I walked around in a daze for weeks afterward waiting for the song."

"I know." I looked for my own mother. There she was, sitting on a purple, grown-up chair outside the children's story room, listening to a book on quilt making.

"Truth is," the woman said, "I thought Mother might be right; there might actually *be* something wrong with me. That's why it was so good to meet the Dragon Charmer."

I felt as if my ears had blinked. "Excuse me, but who did you meet?"

"A Dragon Charmer. He was a wonderful old man—very special. Unique, you might say." The woman smiled. "I guess he should have been. Only a handful of Dragon Charmers are born in each generation."

"Oh," I said.

"Dragon Charmers are very important, you know. We are all that stands between dragons and extinction."

"Are you a Dragon Charmer?" My head felt dizzy.

"Yes," said the woman. She laid one pale, crooked finger on each of my shoulders like a queen bestowing knighthood. "And so are you."

2

ARSON WELLES

I took a step away from her. My heart was beating loudly inside my ears. I was not sure I wanted to hear anything more this strange woman had to say.

I clutched my vox-books to my chest and looked again to my mother. She glanced up from her quilt making book and smiled.

"Of course, you may choose *not* to accept the job," the Dragon Charmer said.

"I may?"

"Oh, yes. Others have refused before you."

"Really?"

"Three others before you, as a matter of fact, in my lifetime."

"What happened to them?" I read everything I could, so I knew that terrible curses often befell people who tried to run away from magical callings.

"Nothing much. They're quite nice people, actually. One became a bank president; one played golf, and the third was student speaker for her high school graduating class."

"That's it? Their noses didn't fall off? They weren't sentenced to eating broccoli for the rest of their lives?"

"Certainly not," the Dragon Charmer said. "I do believe though, they may have lost a bit of specialized hearing.

5

Nothing drastic. Nothing that would affect their everyday lives."

"You mean they can't hear the dragon's song anymore?"

"I'm afraid not," the Dragon Charmer sighed.

Suddenly she seemed much older than when I'd first seen her. She took a few steps to a nearby table and sank onto a too small chair.

"Oh, I don't say I blame them," she said, resting her elbows on her knees. "It's a difficult thing, being a Dragon Charmer. There are no vacations. No dragon sitters listed in the picto-phone directory when you feel more like cruising the Bahamas than taking care of your dragon."

I laid my vox-books on the table and sat down opposite her.

"You mean, you actually have a dragon of your very own?"

"Well, I'm never quite sure who has who, but yes, Arson is with me now."

"Arson?"

"That's what I call him. Arson Welles. Arson because of his, err...talents and Welles, because I had rather a crush on the twentieth century actor, Orson Welles, when I was young—long before your time. In my opinion, there was never anyone quite like Mr. Welles, and there's no other dragon quite like Arson. So, that's what I call him. You could change it, I suppose."

I swallowed the lump of excitement in my throat. "Do you think I could see him? Arson, I mean."

"I can show you only you *after* you have chosen."

"And if I choose *not* to be a Dragon Charmer? Will you *still* show him to me?"

"Yes, but I can't promise you will be able to see."

6

"All right," I agreed. "Please, tell me everything."

The Dragon Charmer settled her long skirts about her knees and patted the pockets of her bright green jacket as if reassuring herself that everything was in its place. Then she began:

"As you know, the world used to be full of dragons. Glorious creatures of all colors and shapes and with all sorts of talents. Unfortunately, only the ones who caused mischief showed up in legends."

"I'd hardly call eating babies for breakfast 'mischief,'" I protested.

"That old tale? Everyone's heard that one (and it's highly exaggerated I must say). But even if it were true down to the last infant, that was only *one* dragon; just as Jack the Ripper was only *one* man. You wouldn't go around trying to kill all men because one turned out to be Jack the Ripper, would you?"

"No, I see what you mean," I said.

"At any rate, people began to think that the mean dragons were the only kind of dragons there were. No one stopped to think about the dragons that kept the clouds moving along with the breeze from their wings, or the ones that melted winter snows with fire from their nostrils. And they never considered how lonely and silent the world would be without the dragons' songs."

"So people like St. George and King Arthur and the rest set out to rid the world of dragons?" I asked.

"Precisely. And they very nearly got the job done. But there was one far-sighted wizard who could see where all this dragon prejudice was leading. This wizard established the Society for the Preservation of Dragons, in the sixth century. Also known as Dragon Charmers."

"Merlin?"

"No, his apprentice, Maxine."

I shook my head. "I never heard of her."

"No one has. And for good reason. In Maxine's time Dragon Charmers had to keep low profiles or else knights ran them through with swords." The Dragon Charmer pretended to thrust a sword at me.

A quick sharp pain pierced my chest.

"Later, when we came to the new world, Puritans drowned us in dunking buckets," the woman continued, "or burned us at the stake when they suspected who we were and what we were protecting."

A small bubble of fear formed in my stomach. "Is it still dangerous, being a Dragon Charmer?"

"Dangerous? Yes, I suppose it is. Not because of knights or witch hunters. No those have been replaced by laws and public officials. The 'no pets' law, for instance: a million dollar fine and three years in prison for keeping a pet. Preposterous. Truly. Not that one would ever consider Arson a pet. Of course not, he's a completely independent being. Except for a few minor details, that is. But also because ordinary people, otherwise perfectly nice people, can not hear the dragon song, nor see the dragon for what it is. These people don't understand when we stop to listen—to relish the unique joys of dragonhood. Sometimes, while we're listening, we appear lazy to them or irresponsible."

I thought of a time I'd stopped to listen.

"I heard the song at school once. Mrs. Kinsey sounded the buzzer on my desk because she thought I was sleeping. I had to serve a detention."

The Dragon Charmer smiled. "Then there are the things we feel like doing *after* we've heard the song. People almost never understand those. We seem foolish."

"Yes, at lunch recess I sat by Willie Raimer. No one ever sits by him—they say he stinks. But he didn't smell so bad to me. It's only the garlic necklace he wears under his uniform shirt to ward off vampires and the like."

"Very sensible of him," the Dragon Charmer approved.

I wasn't in the mood to get into Willie and his theories on vampires.

"I shared my sandwich with him."

"You did?" asked the Dragon Charmer. "What day was that?"

"It was Thursday, last week," I said.

The Dragon Charmer slipped an old-fashioned red leather book from an inside breast pocket of her jacket. On the front cover of the book in large, fancy gold letters was written *Official Dragon Chart Book*. She opened it and ran a finger along an intricate diagram of a fabulous looking dragon.

"Ah, here it is. Arson gained a feather scale on his left wing that day, at 12:17 pm. Would that be your lunch hour?"

"Yes," I said.

"And would your name happen to be Elizabeth Cady DuLac?"

"Yes."

"A very strong name after an excellent woman! Delighted to meet you, Elizabeth."

"I'm called Cady," I said.

"Cady it is, then. I'm Natalie Mondieu." The Dragon Charmer held out her long fingered hand.

"Nice to meet you, too," I shook her hand, which felt light enough to be made of bird bones. "But I don't understand. How did my sandwich and Willie Raimer get Arson a new feather scale?"

"Dear me. Here I've rattled on and on and haven't told you the most important part."

3

Alive!?

Natalie drew herself up to her considerable height and recited.

"Until such time as it is safe for dragons to live openly in the world again, said dragons may grow no more than one scale at a time, and *only* at such times as a human performs an extraordinary act of kindness. Said act must be not only kind, but also brave, and must *not* be performed for the sole purpose of increasing dragon size. Furthermore, and to wit, the party performing said act must receive no compensation for its enactment."

She relaxed again in her chair.

"It sounds legal," I said.

"Oh, it is. It's 'The Dragon Charmer's Code.' The main thing to remember is that last part. It means the person can gain nothing of a material nature from the kindness. So, if Willie had given you a quarter in exchange for your sandwich, it wouldn't have helped the dragon at all."

"I see. But I didn't feel particularly brave, either, when I was sharing my lunch with Willie," I said.

"My dear Cady, you mustn't think bravery has only to do with rescuing people from burning buildings or leaping out of airplanes."

"It doesn't?"

"No, it can also be daring to make friends with people no one else likes. Caring about those people means you risk sharing their loneliness. That is one of the bravest deeds on Earth. It is also one of the most rare."

"Then dragons must grow extremely slowly."

"Oh, yes. Why I've had my dragon for one hundred fifty-one years..."

"One hundred and fifty-one years?" I interrupted. "That means you must be...."

"Ah, ah, ah," Natalie waggled a finger at me. "It is impolite to ask a grown-up's age."

"Excuse me."

"As I was saying, Arson has only grown an inch or so in all that time. He was the size of a caterpillar when the old Dragon Charmer passed him to me, and now he's almost as long as a small chameleon. Still, we hold the growth record for the past two centuries in the western hemisphere," she said proudly. "Of course, I was fortunate to have the deeds of such people as Eleanor Roosevelt, Dr. Martin Luther King, and Brian Delano Dulac counting for my dragon. We never could have done it otherwise."

"Brian Dulac? He's my father."

"He is? You must be very proud of him. Such a remarkably kind man. So brave."

"I am," I said, around a huge lump in my throat. "At least I was. He's gone, you know."

"Gone? Where?"

"He, he..." I commanded myself not to cry. Time to get on with it. Get over it. "My father died."

Natalie's face went pale as milk. "Oh, Cady, I'm so sorry. You and your mother are very brave to come out so soon afterward."

12

"Soon?" I blinked back tears. "He died last December in the big commuter-rail crash. It's been almost a year."

"A year? Really? This *is* confusing. Why I could have sworn that just a few days ago..." she opened her book and ran a finger over the dragon diagram. "Yes! Here it is. Tuesday, October eighth, Brian Delano DuLac earned a dragon chest scale. Those are very difficult to earn, it takes an unusually valorous deed to secure a chest scale—they're so large you see."

"October seventh? But that is just...may I see that book please?"

The Dragon Charmer swiveled the old fashioned book to face me. She pointed out on the diagram the date she'd read. There it was marked plainly in green ink, one dragon chest scale labeled *Brian Delano DuLac, 5:36 p.m., Tuesday, October 8, 2080.*

Day before yesterday.

4

Decision

My hands trembled. Could it be possible? After all of the days and weeks and months of pain, of believing my father dead, that he was truly alive?

The commuter-rail crash had sent several of its cars skyward in flames. The bodies came back in pieces when they came back at all. My father's body was never recovered, but he had been on one of the cars; the ticket records in the commuter-rail reservations computer confirmed it.

For weeks after the crash I believed there was surely some mistake. That the next picto-phone call would be my father, explaining everything away. As the weeks turned into months, I had to admit the chances of that happening were dwindling. And now, I was afraid to hope.

Yet, there was my father's name written in the Dragon Charmer's book. And not only day before yesterday. But on the dragon's wings were more entries. *Brian Delano Dulac, 8:09 a.m., Friday, September 13, 2080,* and *Brian Delano Dulac, 5.33 p.m. Tuesday, June 11, 2080.* And on the dragon's feet, its back, its wondrous spiked tail there were more, dozens of entries in my father's name.

Some entries were for before Father had *died.* In fact, some were dated before I was born. But several were like those on the dragon's wings and chest. According to the diagram, my father, Brian Delano Dulac, was either alive, or the kindest ghost ever. I considered that possibility.

"Has it ever happened that ghosts earned dragon scales?"

"Oh my, no! It would be quite against the code. It specifically states 'human' kindness—not ghosts. Living humans only. No, indeed that would never do."

"So, that means my father is alive."

"Very much alive," Natalie nodded.

"But where?"

She frowned. "I'm afraid I haven't a clue. Except..."

"Except what?"

"Except he must still be on this continent. Dragons can only earn scales from their own areas. And Arson has North America."

My heart sank. "That's it? We can't narrow it down any more than that?"

Natalie shook her head. "Sorry. I guess that isn't much use. But it could be worse. We could have the only dragon in the Western Hemisphere."

"That would be worse."

I ran a finger over the dragon diagram. I could feel a warmth through my skin when I touched my father's name. A tear leaked from my eye onto my cheek.

"I don't know how to thank you," I said.

Natalie took out a bright pink bandanna from her jacket pocket and dabbed the tear from my cheek.

"Well, you might consider becoming a Dragon Charmer. I know it's a lot to ask. Especially on top of all the other things you have on your mind."

I had almost forgotten about the real flesh and blood dragon in all the excitement over my father.

15

"Would taking Arson help me find my father?"

"I don't see how," Natalie said. "And I'm not sure I could confer charmer status on you if you took Arson hoping to gain from it. It might not work. Dragon Charmers must accept the responsibility from a pure love of dragons and a sincere wish to see them survive."

"I see..."

I wasn't at all sure I met those qualifications. I did love dragons, that much was true. How often I had dreamed of catching just one glimpse of the wonderful creatures I'd studied about all of my life.

I didn't know if I could separate the hope that, somehow, the dragon could help me find Father from the wish to see a dragon for itself. I could no longer be certain my love for dragons was pure and unselfish.

"What if I took the dragon for the wrong reasons?"

"Then the damage King Arthur did to dragons would be infinitesimal compared to the wound you would inflict. For King Arthur merely wounded a dragon's body. You would break its heart."

"But how can I know?" I cried.

Across the library, Sara came bounding out of the story room doors with the other four year olds. She wore a golden construction plastic crown, which slipped down over her eyes with each step. Mother closed her book and swept Sara into her arms.

Now there were mere seconds to decide.

"Cady?" The Dragon Charmer said.

I heard my sister from across the room, "Mommy, today the story was about a beautiful princess..."

"Can you do it?"

"...and a brave knight," Sara said.

"You must decide."

Mother took a step toward me.

"...and a horrible dragon." Sara's eyes were wide with wonder.

She wriggled excitedly in Mother's arms.

"Yes," I whispered. "Yes, I can do it."

Natalie opened her bandanna and peered inside. There was a small flash like a match spark on the book in my hands. I watched as green ink inscribed a dragon chest scale right next to the one with Father's name. The scale read *Elizabeth Cady DuLac, 4:23 p.m., Thursday, October 10, 2080.* I closed the book and placed it on top of my other books.

"Now, open your hands," Natalie instructed.

I opened my hands on the table before me. There was a flurry of wings from the pink bandanna, indigo blue and sun yellow. Tiny dragon claws tickled my palm like dandelion fluff.

I had only a moment to see my dragon. But in that moment, I knew Arson was magnificent. His eyes were like brilliant diamonds set in a noble lion-like head. His wings were fragile and intricate with the newest scales paler than the rest. The chest scale, earned just the moment before, was nearly transparent but gaining in color with each passing second.

Natalie laid her hands on my shoulders, as if helping herself to stand.

Arson tilted his head to one side. Sweet, melancholy notes drifted upward. It was the dragon's farewell song.

"Godspeed, Dragon Charmer," Natalie whispered.

With hardly a rustle from her long skirt, Natalie Mondieu disappeared.

17

5

Nigel Quido

"Don't worry, Arson, I'll take care of you," I promised softly.

Then, carefully, tenderly, I slipped the dragon into my uniform's shirt pocket.

Mother and Sara came for me.

"Did you find what you wanted?" Mother asked.

"Yes," I said. "More than I expected." If only Mother knew.

We walked to the library entrance. One at a time we placed our hands on the "patron identifier" scanner shield and laid our stacks of vox-books on the "items charged" scanner.

I was careful to keep my Dragon Chart Book away from the scanner. The old fashioned Chart Book had no sound chip. Which meant it had to be read with the eyes word by word, and I was afraid it might set off the library's alarm system.

I knew that the library still owned a few of this type of book, but only certain people had access to them. Not that it mattered, all of the really good books had been translated to the biblio-vox system and were available to the common people. That's what the library advertisements said.

Arson wriggled impatiently inside my pocket. I patted him gently and hoped he wouldn't decide to try out his wings.

We were almost through the library doors when a voice hissed behind us.

"Here, here, young woman. What is it you have there?"

A *real* librarian came shushing up behind us and laid his hand on my shoulder. "Making off with a library treasure, are you?" The liquid crystal display tag on the man's suit jacket flashed, *Nigel Quido, Librarian.*

"No, sir."

Mr. Quido, pointed to my Dragon Chart Book. "And I suppose you're going to say a little old lady gave you that antique book for an early Christmas present."

"No, sir, she wasn't little," I said.

"Don't be flip with me young woman! Hand it over!" Mr. Quido held out his fish-white hand for the book.

I hid it behind my back. I couldn't give it up. Father's name was in it, and the dates, and the dragon diagram. What if someone did a kindness and the match spark lit while Mr. Quido peered inside? How would I explain that?

"Really, Mr. Quido, I believe there's been some mistake," Mother said.

"Indeed," said Mr. Quido, "and your young woman has made it!"

"Don't let them put Cady in jail!" Sara cried.

"Hush, Sara, no one's going to jail," Mother comforted.

"We'll see about that." Mr. Quido continued to hold out his hand for the book.

"Cady, dear, perhaps you'd better show Mr. Quido what it is you have."

"But, Mother..."

"Please, Cady."

What else could I do? I brought the leather book from behind my back and laid it in Nigel Quido's outstretched hand.

"Now we'll just see what it is you were trying to sneak out of here." Mr. Quido turned the book around in his hands.

Then a strange thing happened. The book, which had been a rich, dark red in Natalie Mondieu's hands and then in my hands, turned a dirty shade of brown in Nigel Quido's hands. The fancy gold script letters which had spelled out *Official Dragon Chart Book* on the front cover disappeared and were replaced with one word, in ordinary black type—*DIARY*.

"Worse and worse," Mr. Quido said. "You're stealing a diary from our collection!"

"It's mine, I tell you."

Mr. Quido opened the book to its center page. Mother and Sara strained to see what was there. I covered my eyes. I hadn't been a Dragon Charmer for five minutes, and I was already in more trouble than I'd been in the rest of my life.

"What's this?"

I was afraid to look.

"Is this some kind of joke?" Mr. Quido's voice quivered with anger. "Sara broke my Compu-draw set? Ate lunch with Willie Raimer, don't see what all the stink is about?"

20

"Huh?" I opened my eyelids a crack. There, scrawled across the lineless pages, was my own none-to-neat handwriting.

"It's nothing but your own dull diary," Mr. Quido pushed the book back at me, as if it were suddenly slimy.

"It is? I mean, yes, it is. I tried to tell you."

"Well, why'd you go skulking about with it then? Suspicious looking if you ask me."

"I think an apology is in order," said Mother.

Mr. Quido tugged at his jacket lapels. "No, no. She needn't apologize. However, I must insist she *never* bring that thing back here again. We wouldn't want to go through another scene like this, would we?"

Mother's face went red. "We certainly wouldn't. I wonder if we might speak with the library director?"

Mr. Quido's chin quivered. "I hardly think the infraction warrants bothering her."

I could see Mother getting stubborn. All I wanted was to get safely out of the library and home with my dragon. I tugged on her arm.

"Come on Mother. It was just a mistake. Let's go home."

"Yes, Mommy, please. Let's go," said Sara.

"All right," Mother shifted Sara to her left hip and put her right arm protectively around my shoulders. I gathered up the vox-books we'd charged, and together, we walked out into the mild October air.

6

Inspections

I closed my bedroom door and pushed in the chamber lock. Opening the first vox-book, I inserted it into the biblio-vox player. The display terminal flashed a picture of knights around a table, and the story of King Arthur, read by a deep male voice, played through the biblio-vox speakers.

I pressed an ear against my bedroom door, making sure Sara was not listening beyond the thin sheet of vinyl as she sometimes did. When I was absolutely certain I was alone, I gingerly lifted Arson from my shirt pocket. I carried him carefully to my bed and smoothing a square on my rumpled comforter, set him down.

Arson tilted his bright blue head first one way and then the other. Then he opened his small mouth and sang.

The room quickly filled with the piping sounds of mockingbirds and the soft, forgotten cooing of the carrier pigeons. The call of the eagle was there and the mighty trumpeting blast of the mastodon.

I stretched myself out full length beside the dragon and watched him pour his song over the room. I worried, at first, that Mother or Sara might hear Arson and come knocking at my door. But after the first minute or so, I gave up worrying and let the song wash over me like crystal rain.

I lay flat on my back, and Arson flew lopsidedly to sit on my chest. I supposed he must be as interested to see his new caretaker as I was to see him. We gazed at each other intently.

For my part, I was not one whit disappointed. Although Arson measured no more than four inches in length, or in height, he was my idea of the perfect dragon.

His head had wide set ears with tiny yellow tufts of fur-like stuff extending from them. His mouth was like an alligator's. His tail, which equaled the length of its body, was blue with stegosaurus type plates spining up in yellow gold along it.

Arson's front feet were like eagle's claws, and his back feet were like the haunches of a dog. The large patches here and there, where dragon scales had yet to be earned, shimmered translucent under the light from the bedroom lamp.

Arson suffered my examination patiently. When I finished, he began an exploration of his own. He traveled my chest from shoulder to shoulder, clambered up my chin, his claws hurting me no more than those of a three week old kitten. Arson moved tentatively across my face, poking his snout inside my nose. Walking gingerly through the brush like landscape of my eyebrows, he whistled his warm smokey breath against my cheeks.

The vox-book was coming to an end. I realized we must have been looking each other over for more than half an hour. Soon, Mother would call me to supper.

I realized I had absolutely no idea what dragon's eat. (Excluding small children, of course. And the child would have to be minuscule at the largest to fit into Arson's mouth.)

"What do you eat, Arson?" I tickled the dragon on it's chin with my pinky finger.

Arson trilled a note.

"If only I could speak dragonese," I laughed. "I'd have it made. Well maybe the *Official Dragon Chart Book* has a hint."

I rolled onto my stomach and opened the chart book. It fell open naturally to the dragon diagram in the center. I ran my finger over the chest scales containing Father's name. It was almost like standing beside him.

Arson flew up and perched on the highest point of my right ear. I can't lie around her mooning over names, all evening, I thought. Surely, there's more to these pages than the dragon diagram. I turned the fragile paper pages back to the beginning. My Grandmother DuLac had told Sara and me how, when she was a girl, these were the most common types of books. I could hardly imagine it. Think of trees being so plentiful they could be cut up and made into books. Amazing.

I found the page labeled "Table of Contents" in the same green ink and fancy script as the dragon diagram's scale entries. I knew that this page served the same function as the touch sensitive-goto screens of a vox-book.

I found an entry labeled—"Dragon Care and Feeding," which began on page three. I thumbed past the Table of Contents page and past an Introduction page which began, *Congratulations on joining the elite ranks of The Society for the Preservation of Dragons.* I guess they must have had commercials even in King Arthur's time. I went on to "Dragon Care and Feeding."

Dragons, I read, *contrary to popular opinion, rarely eat flesh of any kind. In fact they tolerate only a very few foods. Their favored diet is one of fruits, They are particularly partial to kumquats and pomegranates. For variety they sometimes enjoy munching the leaves of Linden trees.*

Kumquats or pomegranates, in the middle of Illianamo with month-long winter freezes approaching in only a few weeks? And *Linden tree leaves*? I had not so much as seen any tree, apart from the town common where six were surrounded by a high fence, let alone a Linden tree, whatever that was. I doubted there were any still in existence. How was I supposed to manage to feed the dragon these delicacies?

"Cady," Mother called. "Supper. Clean your hands."

"Be right there," I answered.

I closed the book and hid it beneath my pillow. I held open the pocket of my uniform shirt.

"Come on Arson," I whispered. "Time to eat. I don't know why you couldn't like something simple like potatoes. We eat plenty of those."

Arson chirruped and hovered down from my ear into the open pocket. He looked at me so cheerfully, that I was immediately ashamed of grumbling. "Never mind. I'm sure we'll find something you like."

I met Sara on the way to the cleansing room.

"Cady, how come the book changed colors when that mean man took it?"

I felt panic flicker in my chest. "I don't know what you mean, Sara."

"Yes, you do," Sara said. "It was red; then it was brown. How'd you do that?"

"You were seeing things. It was brown all the time."

"Can I see it now?"

"No, you can't see. It's personal," I said, firmly, "Now let me in to clean my hands. Mother is waiting."

Sara stepped aside.

"After supper," she said. "I want you to show me after supper. You promised." Then she turned and raced down the hall.

"I didn't promise," I yelled after her.

Sara stuck a finger in each ear and sang at the top of her lungs.

It was no good. She would claim I'd promised, and when I didn't deliver on the promise, she would go crying to Mother.

I couldn't let that happen. I wasn't sure if Mother would be able to see Arson or the book, or if some magic would prevent her as it prevented Mr. Quido. But I couldn't take the chance. I wasn't ready to explain things to Mother or Sara, yet. I wasn't even sure I could explain things to *myself*.

I slammed the cleansing room door behind me. What did it mean that Sara could see the chart book? Was she a charmer, too? Or was it the innocence of her age that allowed her to see things accurately? Whatever it was, I wished Sara would mind her own business for once!

I passed my hands quickly under the Rad-san Cleanser. Grandmother DuLac remembers when this process was accomplished with water. Imagine.

When my hands turned orange I knew they were clean. I moved them from under the Rad-san, and they returned to their natural color. The joints in my fingers ached a little from the cleansing, but that would pass in a few seconds.

I'd been stupid with Sara. Why hadn't I told Sara that the book had passed through a sort of Rad-san system on the way to Mr. Quido's hands? That would explain how the book had changed colors. She might have believed that. But no, I'd had to claim she didn't see what she

26

had seen. Now I would have to do some pretty fast thinking, or she would be on to me.

I hate lying worse than anything. I'm no good at it for one thing. And for another, once I start it is almost impossible to stop.

Oh well, as Father used to say, (no wait, I thought, as Father *still* says) the thing to do when you don't know what to do is whatever comes next. And what came next was supper. For me, that was simple. But for Arson—

7

New Questions

Arson went to sleep in my pocket. His snores sounded like miniature bagpipe squeals. I was sure Mother would hear and ask me to please stop making rude noises. But she did not seem to notice.

Sara, on the other hand, kept swiveling her head trying to find the source of the noise. "What's that noise?"

"What noise, dear?"

"That noise, like whistling."

Mother listened. "I don't hear any whistling, Sara. Do you Cady?

"Nope," I picked up my fork and dug into supper.

Sara looked at me suspiciously, but there was nothing she could do.

As usual, there were potatoes for supper. Mother served them in their "jackets," and Sara and I ate the whole thing. Besides potatoes we each had a spoonful of raisins.

Since Father had "*died*" and his salary as assistant civil engineer for the Tri-State-Region of Illianamo's water department had ceased, none of us DuLacs had to worry about getting fat.

We had only lived in Illianamo's District 5 for three months when the commuter-rail crash occurred. Father had been transferred from the state level office in Capital City to the county level office in Illianamo, District 5. Which

Which meant he had still been in a probationary period on his new job. The government offices of the Tri-State-Region of Illianamo, as much as it sympathized with us, could not possibly provide the survivor's benefits which Father had fallen two days short of earning.

It took nearly everything Mother earned as manager of the "Handi-Mart" to pay our rent and the power bills. The food bill was one thing she could control. We hadn't actually gone hungry since the crash, but dessert was something that was saved for birthdays and other high holidays.

I managed to secret a thumb-sized chunk of my potato and four raisins in the fold of my napkin. I hoped that Arson's tastes had broadened since the sixth century.

"Remember when Daddy was alive," Sara said as she rolled her last raisin around on her tongue, "and we could have green things to eat and *real* fruit and chicken!"

It was only one of Sara's usual after-supper wishing trips, but, for some reason, tonight I had no patience with it.

"Is that all you miss about him?" I said, angrily.

"Cady, don't be mean to your sister."

"I can't help it. Why can't she miss Father for the piggy-back rides or the made-up bedtime stories, the way he smelled, or the way he tapped his leg when he walked?" I shouted. "Why does she have to miss just the food?"

"I don't *remember* piggy back rides or bedtime stories, Cady," Sara shouted back. Then she started to cry.

"Sara can't help what she remembers," Mother said, as she drew Sara on to her lap.

All of the shouting must have awakened Arson, for suddenly, our tiny kitchen was filled with dragon song.

29

My heart turned over in my chest. I did not think Mother could hear, but Sara was another matter.

I watched Mother comfort Sara. How could I expect Sara to remember? She was only three years old when she'd seen Father last. If he didn't come home soon, she might not even recognize him.

And you, Cady, a voice inside my mind asked. *will you recognize your father?*

Of course I will, I thought. But I knew I was forgetting things, too.

There were days, when the first thing on my mind in the morning was not Father, but a test for school or how to talk Mother into letting me get an after-school job.

The forgetting made me feel ashamed. As if, somehow, I was being disloyal to Father. I knew it also meant I was beginning to heal. Somehow it felt wrong to let go. To go on.

For Sara, who had less of Father than I had, forgetting was happening faster.

Sara quieted. "That's pretty," she said.

"What's pretty, dear?"

"The whistling, Mommy."

"Oh." Mother stroked Sara's hair and sang softly to her. Mother's song and Arson's got all tangled up. I couldn't tell which was which. Together they were even more beautiful than apart.

What about Mother? Had she begun to heal, too? I watched her face, which had been so full of pain in the beginning. It was smoother, still sad and thin, but calm.

I tried to remember the last time I had awakened in the night to the sounds of Mother's soft crying in the bedroom next to me. I realized it had been days, maybe even weeks since I'd heard her cry in the night. Probably even Mother was beginning to forget a little.

What if I showed Sara and Mother what the Dragon Charmer had showed me? What if I told them I knew Father was alive somewhere in North America? Would they be able to see the chart? And if they could see, would they believe?

If they believed, then they would surely hope again. With hope would come fresh pain. New questions. I knew it was true because it was happening to me.

The biggest question of all was—how could Father earn dragon scales with acts of kindness yet allow us, his own family, to suffer and struggle?

Until I could find Father and the answer to that question, I could not tell Mother or Sara *anything*.

Arson finished singing. Sara slept on Mother's lap.

Well, that was one problem delayed for a while at least. Sara wouldn't be after me about the book that changed colors any more that night. But I felt low for having shouted at her.

"I'm sorry," I whispered.

Mother nodded. "It's all right, Cady. You're such a help to me, and I know how hard it is for you. Sometimes I forget to thank you."

I couldn't stand for Mother to appreciate me. Not while I was keeping such an important secret from her. I had to get away quickly, or my resolve would weaken, and I would tell her everything.

I folded my napkin into my fist. "I'm going to take out the trash," I said.

"Thank you," Mother smiled at me. "But be careful. You know I don't like your being out after dark."

31

"I will, Mother. I'll only be in the alley." I picked up the waste container and walked out the kitchen door, down five flights of stairs, to the alley behind our building.

Rad-san dumpsters were lined up in the alley—three per building, like huge, crouching gargoyles. I remembered Father's warning me never to play hide and seek in these. One press of the "dispose" button rendered whatever was inside into a tiny pile of gray ash. And the seals around the doors were so tight, being trapped inside would suffocate any living thing in less than five minutes.

I opened the dumpster door and shook our trash on top of a little mound of gray ash on the floor. It gave me the shivers to think of a person inside one of these, like being inside a monster's mouth.

"Anybody home," I called. My voice echoed off the slick grey walls.

I took Arson out of my pocket and showed him the dumpster. "Don't ever go in one of these, you understand? It could kill you like that." I snapped my fingers in front of Arson's nose.

I shut the dumpster door and checked to make sure it sealed. Then I pressed the red button marked dispose. There was a sound like distant thunder, and I knew the left over bits of three days meals had been reduced to almost nothing. Thanks to the miracle of Rad-san technology.

CHAPTER 8

Dragonese

"Here you go, Arson, try this." I set the thumb-sized potato chunk on my dresser in front of the dragon.

Arson circled the potato like a dog inspecting a skunk. He sniffed, shot out a forked purple tongue toward it and sprang away backwards, ticking in his throat like an antique analog clock.

"It's all right," I said. "It isn't alive, you can eat it."

Arson cocked one glittering eye at me. Then pffft—tiny flames blasted the potato into a cinder chunk.

"Yipes!" I jumped and, grabbing for the water glass beside my bed, I splashed the few remaining drops of precious drinking water over the flaming potato. The water sizzled, sending tendrils of smoke toward the ceiling. I clamped the glass over the potato to keep the smoke from reaching the fire duster system.

"No wonder Natalie called you Arson Welles. Listen, dragon, you can't go around torching things you don't like." I rested my chin on the dresser top so as to be eye to eye with Arson. "We'll work out a code. One flap of your wings, means 'Thank you, but no,' two flaps means, 'Yes, please,' and three means 'I'm crazy about it.' Okay?"

Arson flapped his wings twice.

I blinked. "You understand me?"

"Flap, flap."

33

"Hey, this is great. Now how about a little bite of raisin? It's a fruit. Not a *tree* fruit, like the book says you prefer, but they're good. Loaded with iron." I set the shrively looking raisin in front of Arson's nose.

"Remember, one flap means 'no thank you.' No more flame throwing exhibitions."

Arson circled the raisin as he had the potato. Shooting out his purple tongue he flicked a minuscule piece from the raisin's skin. I could see Arson's jaws moving with each chew. Then blurp, a bubble of smoke puffed from Arson's mouth. A thoroughly mashed and masticated bit of raisin fell on the dresser in a drip of dragon spit.

"Aren't you going to swallow it?"

"Flap."

"You have to swallow it to get the nutrients," I sounded like Mother. "Here, try another bite."

"Flap." Arson turned his tail to the raisin, deftly flicking it off the dresser onto the floor.

"There's no need to make a mess," I scolded. I picked up the raisin and the potato cinder (which had finished smoking) and dropped them in the waste container. "Aren't you hungry?"

"Flap, flap."

"Then why don't you eat?"

Arson stared at me with glittering eyes.

"Ooops, sorry. That wasn't a yes or no question, was it?"

"Flap."

"Well, I'm afraid there'll be nothing more to eat until tomorrow morning. Can you hold out that long?"

Flap, flap.

"Good. Now I want to make a list of all the dragon scales Father has earned since the crash. I don't know if it will do any good, but maybe I can see a pattern of some sort. Want to help?"

Flap, flap, flap, flap, flap, Arson flew to his favorite perch atop my right ear.

I opened the *Official Dragon Chart Book* to the diagram of scales earned and began plotting my father's progress. It was soon apparent that there were too many scales for me to keep track of mentally, so I turned on my computer and began entering the data.

I listed scales by date, earliest first, through latest (day before yesterday) and by time earned. Then I broke down the scales by type, wing, chest, toe, snout, belly, ear. I mixed the data, made bar graphs and charts. I pulled up a calendar and plotted the scales that way.

I worked until Mother called through the door that it was time for bed. I was no closer then to learning Father's whereabouts than I had been hours before. But there was something there. I could feel it, if I could only recognize it.

"Cady, it's late," Mother knocked on the door again, "I'm not calling you a third time. Get ready for bed."

I trudged to the cleansing room, stood in the Rad-san shower and zapped my teeth with the Rad-san dent. Then I went back to my room and fell into bed with dates and scales buzzing around my head.

Arson lay in a circle, toe to tail tip, on my pillow.

"Good night, Arson," I said.

Arson winked one glittering eye at me and soon was snoring his bagpipe snore.

9

A Believer

"Cady DuLac, perhaps you can tell the classes which planet is closest to our sun?" Mrs. Kinsey's face wobbled on the teacher's monitor.

The reception from the broadcast classroom in the Illianamo Central School District building in Capital City 325 miles from Illianamo, District #5 middle school was less than stellar. But that didn't prevent the eagle-eyed Mrs. Kinsey from noticing my distracted state of mind.

I slid out of my chair and stood at attention. "Yes, Mrs. Kinsey."

What had she asked me? I looked around for a clue.

I'd been worrying about Arson and my father (not necessarily in that order) instead of listening to the lesson.

It had been almost four weeks since Arson had torched the potato and spat out the raisin. My luck in finding something Arson would eat since that night had been exactly zip.

I had no idea how long a dragon could survive without eating. The chart book didn't say. But, at that rate, even if dragons had the constitutions of camels, it wouldn't be long until Arson suffered from malnutrition. In fact, I was pretty sure that was exactly what was happening. It had been days since Arson had had the strength to sing.

On the monitor, beyond Mrs. Kinsey's head, spun a hologram of the known solar system. That was something, anyway. There was a good chance that was what the rest of the classes had been discussing while I worried.

"Well, Cady?" Mrs. Kinsey prompted.

Willie Raimer coughed and turned his head in my direction. "MER CUR REE" he mouthed, from behind the hand with which he had politely shielded his cough from the other Illianamo middle schoolers.

"I believe the planet is Mercury," I said, praying that my lip reading skills were up to par.

"That is correct," Mrs. Kinsey said. "Now perhaps if Mr. Raimer is able, after such a timely coughing fit, he can tell us when the first successful unmanned mission to Mercury took place."

I dropped back into my seat. The heat was off me for a moment and on Willie.

Willie stood up under Mrs. Kinsey's gaze.

"Yes, Mrs. Kinsey," but as usual, Willie was looking at his feet and mumbling.

"Please lift your head, Willie, I don't know how many times you need to be reminded. The sensors can't pick up your voice from the floor."

Willie raised his head, with its close cropped kinky black hair, a centimeter. "The first unmanned mission by the United States to Mercury was the Mariner 10 in 1973."

"That is also correct," said Mrs. Kinsey. "You may be excused for thirty seconds to cleanse your hands at the Rad-san. We don't want cold germs ripping through the classroom."

"Yes, Mrs. Kinsey." Willie walked to the Rad-san station at the back of the room. I heard the hum of the cleansing machine.

"And now, who can tell me when the first space colonists were launched?"

37

Hands shot up around the room. I signaled a thanks to Willie as he passed my chair, smelling like the an Italian restaurant.

Willie gave me a freshly sanitized "thumbs-up." Then rubbed away the ache in his brown hands from the Rad-san cleansing.

After about a millennium, Science period ended. I picked up my lunch from my cubicle and headed for the cafeteria. I had to stand in line at the Rad-san, but finally I could sit down and worry in peace. I chose a seat as far away from the rest of the eighth grade class as possible.

Unpacking my lunch, I looked for dragon food possibilities. There was nothing in it that I had not offered Arson at least a million times that month. But I had to try.

I pinched a dragon-sized bite from my soya-bun sandwich and slipped it in my shirt pocket.

"Try this, Arson," I whispered.

Arson opened his mouth, and took a tentative taste.

"Good isn't it?"

He spit a wet lump of soya-bun into my pocket; then turned around once and nodded off to sleep.

Lately, sleeping was all Arson had been doing. The thought that he might not wake up one day kept me awake at night.

"Arson, you have to eat something..."

"Who are you talking to?"

My heart skipped right out from behind my ribs and lodged in my throat. I looked up slowly to see Willie Raimer standing across the lunch table from me.

"Hi, Willie." I tried to swallow my heart without choking. "I was talking to myself. Thanks for helping me out with Mrs. Kinsey."

"That's all right," Willie shuffled his feet and looked around him.

I hadn't noticed before how tall Willie was. He always seemed shorter because he stooped over and pulled in, as if he was afraid of being in someone's way. Looking up at him, I could see he must be approaching six feet tall already.

"Guess, I'd better go," Willie said.

There goes my private worrying spot, I thought. Oh well, it doesn't look as if Arson is in the mood for soya bun anyway.

"Why don't you sit here?"

"Thanks," Willie grinned. Setting his lunch container down across from mine, he folded himself onto the backless lunch table bench. "Hey, you want to trade lunches?"

"Naw, not unless you've got a lunch box full of kumquats."

"Kumquats?" Willie laughed, "No kumquats. Just a couple of pomegranates is all."

"What did you say?" I reached across the table and grabbed Willie's arm.

"I said, I'm fresh out of kumquats, but I've got a couple pomegranates."

"Are you kidding me?"

"Why would I kid about that?" Willie looked at me as if I might be in danger of becoming suddenly violent. "My uncle's company sent him to negotiate a deal in the Middle East, and he brought some back. These are the last two we have. Want to try one?"

"You bet I do!"

"All right," Willie held out a reddish colored fruit a little larger than a hen's egg. It felt firm in my hand.

"What do I do with it, cut it or what?"

"Sure you can cut it. The skin's a little too hard to eat, and it's got lots of seeds. But they're pretty good."

I worked at the pomegranate with a plastic knife but I could hardly manage, my hands were shaking so badly.

"Here, let me," Willie said. Taking the pomegranate from my clumsy fingers, he peeled and halved it deftly, then handed it back.

I laid it on my sandwich box and cut it into dragon-bite size pieces as best I could.

"What are you doing that for? You'll hardly be able to taste those tiny pieces."

"I choke easy," I lied. "Hey, I think I see Mrs. Kinsey, in the flesh."

"Where?"

"Over there," I pointed behind Willie's shoulder. When he turned around to get a glimpse of the teacher who, as far as I knew, never left the Illianamo Capital City, I nudged Arson awake and slipped three pieces of pomegranate into my pocket.

"I don't see her." Willie craned his neck, then turned back to face me. "Hey, what gives? Are you trying to make a fool out of me?"

"No, really, I thought I saw her. Must have been my imagination, or a guilty conscience or something." I could see Willie was getting angry with me. I didn't want that. Sheesh, this was the second time he'd saved my life in one day.

Willie peeled his own pomegranate and halved it.

40

I could feel Arson moving around, checking out the pieces of the strange fruit. Then I heard Arson sucking up the pomegranate, smacking his dragon lips noisily.

"Aren't you going to taste the pomegranate?" Willie asked.

"I did," I lied again. "I loved it."

I was doing some quick calculations in my head. I figured the one pomegranate might feed my dragon for a week, maybe even ten days. Although, Arson had a lot of eating to catch up on, so it might be even less than that. Would the pomegranate stay good that long? I didn't know. But Arson would eat today and tomorrow, that was certain.

"I want my mother and sister to try it, so, I'm saving the rest."

"Oh, then take this half, too." Willie pushed his untouched half across the table at me.

I snatched it like an alley rat pouncing on a rotten peanut. "Thanks."

Arson was clawing at my shirt pocket. He could smell the pomegranate and was on his way to getting more. I picked up another piece and pretended to take it to my mouth, but dropped it just as I passed my pocket. Arson leapt up and snatched it in mid-air.

Willie's deep brown eyes widened. "What was that?"

"What?"

"Don't try to fool me again, Cady, I don't like it," Willie said, setting his jaw.

My mind was whirling. What had Willie seen? Only the movement of Arson inside my pocket, surely. It wasn't possible he could actually *see* Arson. Was it?

"Sincerely, Willie, I don't know what you mean?" I tried again.

41

Willie leaned forward, "I mean, what have you got in your pocket?"

"Oh that?"

He had seen. I had to think quickly.

"It's a lizard," I said. "But don't tell anyone will you? You know the penalty for keeping pets."

"You're crazy. I never heard of any blue liz...."

Then Arson began to sing.

Willie stopped talking. His mouth fell open to about Grand Canyon depth.

CHAPTER 10

A New Ally

Willie's gaping mouth was attracting the attention of the lunch room officer, Mr. Warren. I had to reach across the table and shut Willie's jaw for him. I smiled at Mr. Warren and waved. He retreated to his high stool in the center of the lunch room. Nothing else strange had better happen at our table, or we'd be getting a visit from him.

It was so good to hear Arson singing again; I can't describe it. But I had to go on eating, fighting the blissful, trance-like state the song induced.

One person might get by with an occasional public trip to that mental Shangri-La, but I was pretty certain two people simultaneously on the voyage would invite an investigation. That was something I could not afford.

Fortunately, Arson was too weak from lack of food to sing for long. While Willie was still checked out, I slipped Arson two more bites of pomegranate.

"That will have to hold you until we get home. Okay, Arson?"

Inside my pocket, "flap, flap."

Willie came back to the Illianamo lunch room slowly, by degrees. It was interesting to watch the phenomenon I had been through so many times myself happening to someone else. If this was how I looked, it was no wonder the rest of the world thought I was spatial.

43

It was something like awakening from a deep, fevered sleep. All the muscles in Willie's face twitched back to life individually. His eyes grew warmer and browner and more alive than I had ever imagined they could be.

"Are you okay, Willie?"

"Wonderful," Willie smiled at me, and I knew it was true. "You heard it, too. Didn't you?"

It wasn't so much a question when Willie said it. It was more of a statement. But how much of the truth could I admit without dragging Willie into it?

"Well..."

"How long have you known about them?"

All of my life? Twenty-seven days? I didn't know which to answer. I played dumb. "Them?"

Willie leaned his curly head closer to mine. "Dragons," he whispered.

"Dragons?" My heart was certainly getting its aerobic workout this lunch period without my ever moving a muscle.

Then a light switched on in Willie's mind that I knew I would never be able to extinquish.

"That's what you have in your pocket!"

"Shhhh."

"It is, isn't it?"

"Yes, it's what I have. But keep quiet will you? I don't want the whole middle school knowing."

Although, of course, they couldn't know. At least most of them couldn't. Only a handful born every generation in all of North America, that's what the Dragon Charmer said. What were the chances of two attending the same middle school in the fifth Illianamo school district? Astronomical.

44

Yet, here was Willie, proof positive, that there were two of us. I didn't know what it meant to meet a second one. I couldn't take a chance on a third.

"I never thought they would be so small," Willie said, wonderingly. "Does it shape-shift?"

"Shape-shift?"

"You know, change size? Can it expand? Blow itself up to elephant size if it wants?"

"No," I said. "At least I don't think so. The book doesn't say anything about it. And it's pretty thorough."

"It comes with a book?"

"Yes, one of the old fashioned kind with paper pages and a table of contents—the whole works."

"Wow! Can I see it?"

"The book?"

"Well, yes, and the dragon."

"Arson? I don't know."

"Is that it's name?"

"That's what Natalie Mondieu, the Dragon Charmer who gave him to me, called him. Arson Welles. You know, after the actor."

"It's a boy dragon?"

"I think so. I wouldn't know how to tell, really. It seems like a boy."

"This is terrific!"

"Well, yeah, it is. But you've got to calm down. Mr. Warren is watching us.

Willie didn't calm down. Instead he snapped his fingers so loudly it sounded like a firecracker popping.

"That's why you're saving the pomegranate. Your dragon, I mean, Arson, likes them, doesn't he?"

45

Mr. Warren hitched his mammoth frame down from the stool and started our way.

"Yes. Willie, you have got to stop this right now! Mr. Warren is coming."

I thought of the Puritan Dragon Charmers and their dunking stools and the medieval knights' spears through the heart. Those punishments seemed like child's play in comparison to the power Mr. Warren wielded.

I checked the digital time display on the lunchroom wall. One more tick and the bell signaling lunch termination would sound. I gathered up my uneaten sandwich and stuffed it inside my lunch container. I brushed crumbs into my hand and mopped up pomegranate juice with my uniform sleeve.

At last the bell sounded. As I stood up, Willie caught me by the arm.

"I *have* to see him."

I believed Willie. There was a corner of me that was relieved at having someone to share Arson with. But most of me felt nauseated by fear.

"Meet me after school at the library. Three forty-five."

"Three forty-five, at the library," Willie agreed. He let go of my arm, and I brushed past Mr. Warren.

"Good afternoon, Mr. Warren," I said.

"I'm watching you, Miss DuLac."

I know, Mr. Warren, I thought. I know.

11

Old Enemy

Willie looked like a bright eyed maniac.

"Have you got him? Let me see!"

"Shhh!" I hissed and grabbed him by the elbow. "I haven't much time. Mother is expecting me at home. Come over here."

I guided Willie to a table at the back of the children's room between towers of vox-books.

"Where is he?"

"He's here in my pocket. But before you see him, you must know some things and promise some other things."

"Anything!" Willie said.

Then I told him about the problems and perils of being a Dragon Charmer. I told him he must never *ever* let on to anyone that dragons still existed. I made him swear on his eyes to keep Arson's secrets.

Willie crossed his heart. "I swear, Cady, they could kill me, and I wouldn't give you away."

"All right. I believe you," I said.

What choice did I have? I opened my pocket and signaled Arson to come out.

Arson peeked his head out first and then, with a flip of his tail, he was perched on the palm of my hand.

47

Willie was speechless. He held his own hands cupped together, palms up, and Arson flew into them without a second's hesitation.

I felt a stab of jealousy that Arson would leave me so easily at Willie's first invitation. After all we'd been through together, Arson could at least have wondered if I minded his leaving me.

Willie brought Arson up to eye level and examined him closely.

"He's amazing!" Willie said, at last.

"Yes, he is"

"He has such beautiful colors in some places, and in others it's almost as if I can see through him."

"Those scales haven't been earned yet." I explained about the chart book and the process for earning dragon scales.

"I see." Willie was the smartest boy in our school. He didn't miss anything.

"What about this part here on his nose? Not quite a color— not quite translucent."

"That must be a new one," I said. I opened the chart book to the diagram. "Yes, here it is. Well, how about that?"

"What?" Willie craned his neck to see. I swiveled the old-fashioned book so Willie could have a better look at the inscription. It read—*William Douglas Raimer, 11:13 a.m., Wednesday, November 7, 2080.*

"Hey, what gives? That's my name."

I shrugged. "Must be when you helped me out with Mrs. Kinsey."

"Well, if that doesn't take the cake. Let me see if my name's on here any other times." Willie took the book and placed it squarely in front of him.

Arson flew back to me and landed on top of my right ear.

"Hey, little guy." Willie made as if to catch Arson, then thought better of it and went back to examining the diagram. "Yeah, here I am again, on the belly, and here on the toe. You mean to say all these different days I was doing something to earn a dragon scale, and I never even knew it?"

"That's the way it works," I said.

"And here's your name, too. You're on here lots of times. And isn't this your father? But I thought he was...." Willie looked up stunned.

"Do you know what this means, Cady?"

"Yes."

"Wow! That's great! But where is he? Is he hiding out or something? He got people after him?"

Willie was speaking the questions out loud that I had asked myself a million times in the past month.

"I don't know, Willie," I confessed. "And I don't know how to go about finding out. The only clues I have are the dates and times he earned his scales. I've plotted those every way I know how. I've got about two dozen charts and cross references by now with the information I have. So far nothing seems to add up. The only other thing I know is that he's somewhere in North America because Arson can only get scales earned on this continent."

"That's it?" Willie scratched his chin.

"That's it."

"Not much to go on, is it?"

49

"No, it isn't."

"Well, we'd better get cracking then, if we have the whole of North America to cover," said Willie.

"What do you mean?"

"It's pretty simple, really. First we have to make some basic deductive hypotheses about the reasons your father has gone missing. You know, look at his life, his work. If he has any enemies...."

"Father? Enemies?"

Willie nodded. "Sure, why else would he stay gone this long—unless he had amnesia or something and didn't remember where he belonged."

"Amnesia?"

"I don't think that's likely though, do you? I mean it happens in novels and movies and stuff but not too much in real life." Willie rubbed his hands together excitedly like a starving man ready to sit down to a twelve course meal.

"Then we have to rule out the impossible from the highly improbable but possibles, and the probables and possibles until we arrive at what *is*. Then we will know where to begin our search."

"Willie, I have no idea what you're talking about."

"Well, for instance. Where did your father work?"

"He was an engineer for Illianamo, but I don't see..."

A shadow fell across the table where Willie and I sat. We looked up at the same instant. A cold hand gripped my heart. Nigel Quido glared down at us—his fists firmly planted on his skinny hips.

"I thought I told you *never* to bring that book in here again."

12

Caught

Mr. Quido snapped the chart book up from the table. The dragon diagram melted away. Lines from my life in my own handwriting took its place.

Willie saw what had happened. "Hey, what gives?"

I kicked him under the table to keep him from saying anything more.

Arson's claws tightened on the rim of my ear. I turned my head away from Mr. Quido, hoping to keep Arson out of sight. Quido couldn't see the book for what it was; did that mean he wouldn't see Arson either? I didn't want to find out.

"Perhaps you'd like to donate this book to the library's antique collection," Quido said. "Perhaps that is why you can not remember to keep it away from here."

"No, sir," I said.

"What?" Mr. Quido's voice was cold. "Do me the courtesy of looking at me when you speak to me, young woman."

I moved my head imperceptibly and squinted at Quido through the tail of my left eye. "I said, 'no, sir.' Sir," I repeated.

"What are you hiding now?" Quido's free hand shot out. Grabbing my chin in his bony fingers, he jerked my head around to face him.

I felt Arson slip from my ear top and slide all the way down to my shoulder.

"What's this?" Quido made a grab for Arson. "What sort of slimy creatures are you smuggling in here?" He held Arson by the tail between his index finger and thumb.

"Stop that, you'll hurt him!" I shouted.

"A chameleon? Ugh!" Mr. Quido held Arson higher in the air and as far away from himself as possible.

"I'm sure you are aware of the penalties for owning pets. Add to that smuggling one into a public institution. I am forced to turn this whole matter over to the director."

Quido took a step away from us. The chart book, now brown and ordinary, was in his left hand, and Arson, wriggling by a chameleon's tail, was in his right hand.

"NOW!" Willie shouted.

"What?"

Willie leaped from his seat and threw a full body tackle on Mr. Quido, who went down with a whoosh of air and a echoing thud. The chart book skittered across the floor. Arson flew through the air without wings.

Without thinking, I planted my foot on Quido's backside and launched myself after Arson. I caught Arson in mid-air and landed again on my feet by Quido's right hand. Fingers clutched my ankle. I jerked free and ran.

I calculated the chances of retrieving the chart book, but it was too far away. I would have to get out of there and fast! I gave the book up for lost, and sprinted through towers of biblio-vox books on either side of me.

Out of the Children's Room. Past the patron identifier stations. I slid under the restraining mechanical arms of the detection system and heard the alarm set up its eardrum-piercing din.

I ran blindly. Feeling footsteps pounding behind me, I didn't dare look back.

I raced up the street in the direction of home. Then an alarm as deafening as the library's system sounded in my mind. "Don't go home," the alarm warned. "Quido knows your name. Quido has seen your family. That is the first place he will look."

My feet turned automatically down an alley way I'd never before taken. Rad-san dumpsters loomed on either side of me, hulking like huge brown monsters ready to burn me to ashes. At the end of the alley stood a brick wall. The only way out was back the way I had come.

"Which way?" I heard a thundering voice from the street I'd just left.

"In the alley," another voice answered.

I opened a dumpster in the middle of the line and stepped inside. I remembered my father's warnings. But I had no choice.

It was as good as committing suicide by incineration if anyone punched the button marked "dispose" on the outside of my dumpster. It was as good as slipping a plastic bag over our heads and tying red ribbons at our necks if anyone merely noticed the door ajar and shut it.

If we were discovered, Arson would certainly be taken from me. My family would be held responsible for the million dollar fine, I would go to juvenile jail and Arson would be held in some kind of pet prison, where he might live out his days disguised as a chameleon.

"I'm sorry, Arson," I whispered.

What a horrible way for a dragon to die.

13

Air

"Check all these Rad-sans," the first voice said.

Down the alley, dumpster doors popped as their seals were broken and the searchers peered inside. I listened to the sounds come closer and closer.

I scoured my mind for some kind of plan, but I was nearly numb with terror. Nothing helpful occurred to me.

I felt the vibrations through the dumpster's wall as the door next to mine was forced open then slammed shut. The sound like thunder rolled, and I knew the searcher had pushed the 'dispose' button. Had it been habit or frustration that made him activate an empty dumpster? Did they have orders: "get the kid, dead or alive?"

That was it. We were next.

I set my feet and steeled my legs to bolt against whoever was on the other side of my door. With luck, I could knock him down and run back out of the alley into the street.

What if the second voice I'd heard was ready to grab us? I couldn't think of that, or I would do nothing—give up. I couldn't afford that. There was no "Olly, Olly Oxen Free" in this game of hide and seek.

I heard the latch on the dumpster handle push in. I readied myself then...

"Hey! We got her out here!" A third voice shouted down the alley way. "Come on! Hurry!"

The latch on my door released, and whoever was outside gave it a mighty shove. The Rad-san dumpster door popped shut with a snick of the seal. I waited for the searing, thundering heat of the Rad-san disposal blast. It did not come.

I breathed and realized I had been holding my breath. We were not discovered.

But Arson and I were trapped inside the dumpster in absolute darkness with only a few minutes of breathable air. I forced my mouth closed to keep from screaming.

Listening to the sounds of running footsteps die in the alley, I tried to think of a way out.

There was no door handle on the inside of the dumpster. But if I could find something sharp inside, something the rad-blasts had failed to reduce to ash, I might be able to wedge it into the door seal. Even if I couldn't open the door completely, perhaps I could break the seal to let in enough outside air to keep us from suffocating.

I felt the slick walls of the dumpster inch by inch with my hands. Nothing.

With Arson in his favorite perch on my ear, carefully, I knelt on the floor. There was barely enough room for me to kneel down. My head was against the door, my feet against the back wall. I ran my hands through the ashes which covered the floor. Commanding myself not to panic, not to hurry, I probed every inch of the floor. Nothing.

How many minutes had I used. Two, maybe. Three? How many minutes did we have left?

"I'm sorry, Arson," I said. "I don't know what else to do. If we could only break the seal a little then we might live long enough for someone to open the door. But there's nothing sharp enough in here."

I felt light headed. Our oxygen supply was running low.

Pffft. Arson shot a miniature flame from his mouth. For one instant I could see where the seal fitted between the door frame and the dumpster wall. It looked possible. I found the seal with my fingers.

"Can you give me another light, Arson? If I could just see better."

Pffft.

Hurriedly, I clawed at the seal like a desperate animal. My bitten down nails failed to leave even the slightest marks. I kept on digging.

Arson flew from my ear onto my hand.

"Arson, you'll have to move. I can't dig with you on my fingers. You'll fall."

Pfffft, pfffft, pfffft. Arson shot consecutive flame blasts at the seal I had been working on.

The dumpster seal was designed to withstand tremendous amounts of heat. Of course it was a different sort of heat, disbursed at a different level and concentrated on the floor of the dumpster not on the seal itself. I let Arson go on working, even though I knew his fire burned up our oxygen supply at an even greater rate than breathing alone.

Pffft, pffft, pffft. Arson continued his assault on the door seal for perhaps thirty more seconds. Then he flew back and perched on my wrist.

I felt for the section of seal Arson had blasted. It wasn't difficult to locate. It was searing hot to the touch. But more importantly, it was *soft*!

I dug with my fingers at the square inch Arson had worked on. Blisters raised on my fingertips almost immediately. The super-heated seal stuck to my skin. But I knew it was dig or die, so I dug.

I dug until the inch of softened seal was completely gone. Something wonderful happened. I felt a tiny trickle of cool November air from the alley way outside. Would it be enough?

I was breathing in shallow, hyperventilating gulps from the desperate work of breaking the seal. I stuck my mouth to the tiny gap and swallowed air. It made me cough and splutter. I felt my heart rate slow to a gallop.

"Your turn." I moved Arson closer to the tiny opening. I could feel him contract and expand with each deep, delicious breath.

"We'll rest for awhile. Then we'll make another hole. Okay, Arson?"

"Flap, flap."

14

Freedom

Besides air, the tiny space let in a pinhole of dusky light. It wasn't much, but it was something.

My blistered fingers smarted all the way to my elbows. The thought of digging through more molten seal made me want to cry. For now, all I wanted was rest. I sat flat on the dumpster floor, crossing my legs American-Indian style. Just a few minutes, I thought, and then I'll get back to business.

Business... the word trailed off in my mind like the last knot of a kite's tail.

Resting my head against the dumpster door, I tried to think about what Willie had said in the library. If my father had enemies it had to be because of his business. But what enemies could an engineer for the tri-state government make?

All right, first things first. If Father's disappearance had to do with business, then he must be (as unlikely as it seemed to me) some sort of threat to someone powerful. So, what was Father working on when the commuter-rail crash happened?

That was easy. He was working on what he had always worked on. Water purification.

Most of the old fashioned uses for water—cleansing bodies, washing clothing, cleaning buildings—had been replaced by Rad-san technology. The one thing for which there was no substitute was drinking water. Supplying even the minimum amount of safe drinking water for each person was a difficult and time consuming task.

My father (along with all of the other engineers and researchers in the water division) was constantly searching for better ways to clean the water supplies. How could that earn him enemies?

It made no sense to me. The longer I thought about it the less I understood it.

The blisters on my fingertips throbbed. As much as I dreaded it, I knew it was time to make another assault on the seal.

"Listen, Arson, this time lets try digging out the spot where the handle latches. If we break through there we might be able to release the door from the inside," I said.

Arson agreed.

I breathed in as much air as I could from the tiny break we'd managed before and rose again to my knees. There was no sure way of telling exactly where the door handle was from the inside, so I made my best guess.

"I think it should be about here." I raised Arson on my palm to kneeling shoulder height. "Okay, do your dragon thing."

Pffft. Arson blasted the seal at the new level. I tried not to think about what I would do if this was not the right latch level. It would be a new hole, I told myself, no matter what. A new hole meant more air.

Arson worked at the seal. After a couple of minutes I could see it beginning to soften.

"Give it another shot. Then I'll go to work." My fingers said I couldn't, but what did they know?

Arson drew in breath to give the seal one more blast.

"Cady."

I thought I heard my name called. It couldn't be. No one knew I was here. Unless the searchers were back. I didn't dare dig at the seal for fear of being heard.

"Go away!" I silently commanded whoever it was.

The voice came again. "Cady?"

The word came through odd and muffled, like echoes in a glass sphere. It sounded like...

"Willie?" I wasn't sure if I'd spoken out loud or only thought it.

There was a knock on the dumpster door next to mine.

"Cady?"

It was Willie! Even through the thickness of walls I knew it was him.

"Over here, Willie. We're trapped inside." I thumped twice on our dumpster door with the heel of my hand. "Let us out." I whispered as loud as I dared.

"Hold on. I'll get you out."

I heard Willie's hands grasp the handle on the outside of the dumpster. I felt the vibration as the handle turned and snicked back the latch.

Willie snatched the door open. I fell headlong into the alley, scraping my already battered fingers on the rough pavement. Arson, at least, had presence of mind to take flight while I fell.

Willie grabbed me under both arms and hauled me to my feet. "You look terrible!" Willie said.

"Thanks." I couldn't believe he had gotten away. But I was in no shape and had no time to ask him the particulars.

"We've got to get out of here. They'll figure out I tricked them and be back here looking for you any minute." Willie looked at me doubtfully. "Can you walk?"

"I can do better than that." I held open my shirt pocket. Arson flew inside.

"Good, then follow me," Willie said.

He set a loping pace back down the alley and into the street. I followed close at his heels.

15

Fugitives

We did not stop running until we reached Willie's apartment complex. Willie let us in with his indenta-card which hung on a string around his neck along with three clumps of garlic.

"My parents won't be home from hospital rounds for hours, yet," Willie said. "We've got the whole place to ourselves. I'll see what I can round up for us to eat."

I dropped down on Willie's living room sofa. Every muscle in my body decided to tremble at once. I never wanted to be this scared again. I couldn't go home. I couldn't go to school. I wasn't even sure how long I would be safe at Willie's.

I was a fugitive.

Suddenly, I realized, if our theory was correct, this was exactly the life my father had been living for the past ten months. No sane person would elect this sort of life without good cause.

Arson flew from my pocket and landed on the coffee table. I took out a few pieces from the half pomegranate I'd wrapped and stored in my pant's pocket.

"Hungry, Arson?" I laid the pieces of fruit in front of Arson.

It occurred to me, Arson's whole life had been a fugitive's life—always hiding. Constantly needing protection from a world in which he was absolutely unwelcome. Condemned to masquerading his true self to the world at large during his brief and occasional releases from hiding.

I had taken on the responsibility for Arson's safety with no genuine understanding of the enormity of the task. So, for the rest of my life (or until I found another Dragon Charmer) some portion of my life would be secret and furtive.

Was this what Natalie Mondieu had endured: blistered fingers and frantic chases down blind alley ways? She should have told me!

Willie returned with a plateful of peanut-butter and soya sandwiches. I wondered whether I would be able to eat. But once I got the first bite down, I discovered that unbridled fear made me ravenous.

I held the soft sandwiches between the ball of my thumb and the first knuckle of my index finger to spare my throbbing finger tips. Between bites I told Willie what I'd been thinking about just before he'd rescued us from the dumpster. I told him what Father had worked on for the whole of my life—water purification.

"I just can't imagine how Father's work could have anything to do with his disappearance." I finished the last bite of my second sandwich and reached for a third.

Willie leaned back in his chair, licking a drop of peanut butter from his middle finger.

"That's very interesting," he said.

"I'm happy you think so," Willie's casual attitude towards my father's situation was beginning to get on my nerves.

"Let's look at this picture logically. Your father worked on cleaning up our water supplies to make them drinkable. He used the current system to accomplish this.

In addition, he experimented with new and different systems which might accomplish the task better. Did your father ever patent any of the systems he invented?"

"No. He thought he was close to a better system a couple of times. Then something always went wrong."

"Did that depress, him? When things went wrong, I mean."

"Well, sure, a little. But then he'd always quote Edison—something about, 'now that we know what doesn't work we're closer to finding what will.' Father agreed with that. He believed even failures taught him something important."

"I like it," Willie said. "So, your father got close several times, but no cigar. Suppose after twelve years of eliminating the 'won't works' he came up with the all time, number one, queen mother of water purification systems."

"Well, that would be great! Who wouldn't be happy about that? No more rationing drinking water."

"Yeah, but what if his system was *so good*, it meant not only more drinking water, but water enough for everything." Willie's eyes shone with the possibilities.

"Everything?"

"Yeah, everything. Clothes, bodies, dishes...."

"But we wouldn't ever go back to water for those things, would we?" I said. "Doesn't the Rad-san way destroy more germs than soap and water?"

"Sure, more germs, more bone marrow, more muscle tissue, more fabric fiber. You name it Rad-san destroys it. Why do you think your hands hurt after a Rad-san cleansing?"

"That's just a temporary tingling sensation, letting you know all the germs have been destroyed."

"Cripes, Cady, you sound like a Rad-san commercial," Willie snapped. "Look, you've got a grandmother, right?"

"Right."

"What do her hands look like?"

"Well the fingers are crooked and she rubs them a lot. Her knees hurt her, too and her back. That's because she's old."

"How old is she?"

"Fifty-six."

"I've got news for you Cady, unless your Grandma has a particular disease naturally, she shouldn't be having any of those symptoms, *yet*."

"But *all* the people her age look like that."

"Exactly! And all the people her age have been using the Rad-san cleansing system for the bulk of their adult lives."

"But if the government knows that Rad-san is bad for us, why do they let us use it."

"At first they didn't know. By the time they *did* know, we'd messed up our water supplies so terribly with chemicals and just plain garbage, there was nothing else available to clean things up with. And the diseases from germs are as bad or maybe worse than what Rad-san does." Willie spread his hands and hunched his shoulders. "It was a no-win situation."

"So, you think people from Rad-san blew up the commuter-rail to get my Father?"

"I'm only saying it's a logical possibility."

"But the Tri-State government caught the terrorists who did it. The Populist's Freedom Force claimed responsibility."

"Sure, and two flunkies nobody ever heard of before got sent away to Polar Prison, never to be heard from again. And Populist's Freedom Force suddenly has money from untraceable sources."

"You don't *know* that for sure," I said.

"No, I don't *know* anything for sure. But it's a darned good guess."

I shook my head trying to take it all in. Arson, finished with his pomegranate snack, flew back to my knee. I didn't see how it could be that something I'd trusted in my whole life could be *bad* for me.

"How do you know all this about what Rad-san does to us?"

Willie looked me in the eye. "My parents are doctors. They see what 'cleansing the Rad-san way' does, every day."

"But you know it and you *still* use it." I heard an accusing note in my voice.

This was the boy who only an hour before had rescued Arson and me from the dumpster, bringing the number of times he'd snatched my soya buns from the fire that day to a grand total of three. Yet, at that moment, I felt he was a bigger traitor than Benedict Arnold ever considered being.

Willie shook his head. "I only *pretend* to use it most of the time. Like today in the classroom...." Willie popped a length of plastic from his long-sleeved uniform shirt. "I stick this piece under long enough for the cleanser to make its sound—that's it. Then I'm outta there."

"But if you don't cleanse...."

"Oh, I do. Just not very often. Once a day, tops for my hands. Every other week a full body cleansing," Willie said. "That's what the garlic's for. It masks other

66

odors and it keeps people at arm's length. It's very effective; you should try it."

"No vampires?"

"Naw, that's the chump story. You didn't fall for that did you?"

I felt my neck flush right up to my ears.

"Of course I fell for it. I've fallen for every other chump story that came along. Rad-san cleansers are good for you, Father died in a rail-crash, Willie Raimer believes in vampires,—why wouldn't I believe it? I'm the regular chump of the week!"

"Hey, hey. Simmer down. We can't waste time getting mad at each other. We have to figure out what to do."

"Sure, right," I said.

But I felt deflated—like a kid's balloon with a pin hole—the air was leaking out of me. I had to be the stupidest person on planet Earth.

16

A Pattern

"If only I hadn't lost the chart book," I said. "There was something in there to help us. If I could see it one more time I know it would click."

Willie jumped to his feet and made a salaam. "Your wish is my command, oh great and powerful Dragon Charmer."

He whipped the chart book from the neck of his now unbuttoned uniform shirt and presented it like a treasure on the palms of both hands.

"How did you get that?" I reached for it automatically but my ruined fingertips cried out in pain when they touched the hard cover of the book. I drew them back and tucked them in my arm pits.

"It was simple. I jumped over old Quido, lying there writhing in agony and calling for library security, and scooped it up. Down my shirt it went and no one was the wiser."

"You'll have to turn the pages for me," I said, "I don't think I can."

"Sure thing." Willie sat down beside me on the couch. The chart book fell open naturally to the dragon diagram.

"It smells like garlic," I complained.

"Don't be picky," he replied. "Now what in here is it we're looking for?"

"This is the page we need," I said. "On the day Arson came to live with me, I made up charts from Father's dragon scale dates and times. I thought there might be a pattern that would help me locate Father."

"Very logical of you," Willie approved.

"Thanks. But the charts are home in my computer. We'll have to do the work over again."

"So be it." Willie snapped open a hand held computer the size an envelope and pushed the "on" switch. "Now, are we looking at *all* of the dragon scales earned by Brian DuLac or did you narrow them down somehow?"

"At home I did both. But I think we should concentrate on the period after he was *killed*."

"Gottcha!" Willie bent over the book and began entering data. When he finished he had a table that looked like this:

Day	Date	Time
Tuesday	12/26/79	8:08 A.M.
Tuesday	1/2/80	5:17 P.M.
Thursday	1/25/80	8:05 A.M.
Thursday	2/1/80	5:14 P.M.
Tuesday	3/5/80	8:10 A.M.
Tuesday	3/12/80	6:14 P.M.
Thursday	4/18/80	8:04 A.M.
Thursday	4/25/80	5:11 P.M.

The chart went on like this right up through October.

"Well," Willie said, "I'd say there is definitely a pattern. Whatever kind and brave thing your father is doing he's doing it like clockwork on successive Tuesdays and Thursdays."

"Yes, I saw that before, but it doesn't' tell us *what* it is he's doing or where." I stared at the computer chart.

"I have to hand it to your father; he's consistent."

"He does adhere to schedules," I said.

"I can see that."

"Hmmmm. I wonder what delayed him on March 12th. Whatever it was didn't happen until almost an hour later than usual."

"Maybe his train was late," Willie joked.

"Of course, that's it!" I jumped up so quickly I spilled Arson off my knee and onto the coffee table. "Sorry, Arson, are you ok?"

"Flap, flap."

"It was a joke, Cady."

"I know, but you're still brilliant. Don't you see that's exactly what this is. It's a schedule. On the 12th of March something held up the usual proceedings. When did we have that heavy snow storm? The second week of March, right? Everything shut down early, remember? That would make trains run late."

"But was it the 12th? And couldn't it be something else? Like breakfast and supper at the homeless mission? Opening and closing at the tree museum?"

"No, it's the commuter-rail schedule. I know it!" I was trembling again, but this time it was excitement making me shake. "Quick, check the chart. Are we ready for a Tuesday scale or a Thursday?"

Willie scanned the chart. "Thursday—looks like a morning deed."

"Tomorrow!" I could hardly breathe.

"But what do you think he's doing?"

"I don't know, Willie. I don't care. All I know is, tomorrow I may see my father."

CHAPTER

17

What If...

Willie cleared a space on his bedroom floor between his bed and the wall for me. He unrolled a sleeping bag and stole a pillow from the living room.

"I'd let you have the bed, but my folks check on me when they come home from the hospital," he said. "They don't actually come in, just look at me from the door, but I'm pretty sure they'd notice the difference between your head and mine. They'll never see you on the floor."

"What about in the morning?" I asked.

"We'll leave before they wake up. I'll write them a note saying I have before school detention. They'll believe that; it happens often enough."

"All right." I slipped inside the sleeping bag with my school uniform still on. Willie had salved and bandaged my blistered fingers, but I couldn't imagine undoing any buttons. The only clothing I removed was my shoes. I thought about leaving them on, too, in case I had to make a run for it again. I was becoming more and more convinced that life as a fugitive was a thousand times worse than any movie director ever portrayed it.

My poor mother would believe she'd lost me as well as Father, now. Had she contacted the police, or would she wait the night through, hoping to hear from me? Had the police already visited her? There was no way for me to find out without putting her and Sara in even more danger.

Arson slipped into his favorite position on my pillow. Soon his whistling dragon snore began. I couldn't imagine how he managed to sleep so well, being on the run constantly. But then he had the advantage of never having known any other way.

Willie slept like a top. Literally. He spun in his bed like the "button on a string" game Grandma DuLac made for me one time. Pull the string—the button whirls. Relax the string—the button twirls. By the time Willie's parents opened the door and peeked in on him a little after midnight, Willie was wound up in his blankets as tightly as a butterfly in its cocoon. Willie was right, apart from the presence of my blonde head where Willie's should have been, they never would have mistaken my rigid body for Willie's.

It would be another sleepless night for me. I was far too excited (not to mention frightened) to sleep. Tomorrow, I would see Father. I was convinced of it. But what if he had changed? What if he were staying away by choice instead of from necessity? No, that couldn't be. Willie was right, it had to be his job. And the fact that he couldn't come home to us, must mean he was still in danger.

What if he was wearing a disguise?

What if I couldn't pick him out of the crowd?

What if I was not the only one watching for him?

What if, even *after* I found him, he wouldn't come home?

What if....

73

The wavering autumn Illianamo sun was peeking through the crescent shaped window of Willie's bedroom before I ran out of "what-ifs" and fell asleep.

18

Spotted

The Illianamo District 5 Commuter Rail Station was exactly like every other commuter-rail station in the Illianamo Public Transit System. It was as if there was an ordinance that no matter which Tri-state area you visited, as long as you were in the rail station, you would feel as though you'd never left home.

The floor was made up of black and white squares laid out in a checkerboard pattern. Rail-pass agents, encased in clear booths, had regular features, and were sharply dressed in the official wine and gold jumpsuit of the Commuter-rail line. There were rows of institutional chairs which were so unsuited to sitting that most commuters never used them.

Commuters milled about by the hundreds, savoring their one ration of coffee from collapsible cups and listening to the Daily-vox news.

Rail security people were about as inconspicuous as Santa Claus in July. They strolled around pointing their portable scanners at any container larger than a medicine bottle. Willie and I blended in about as well as the security people. We were the only non-adults in the station.

Willie bought us two mugs of chocolate drink from a beverage window. We sipped our breakfast, leaning against a wall opposite the hologram map of the commuter-rail stops for this line.

"You're sure we're due for a morning deed?" I asked for about the millionth time.

"Yes, aren't you?" Willie answered, grumpily.

"Sorry," I took another sip of the chocolate and felt the caffeine hit the bottom of my empty stomach. "I'm nervous is all. What if he doesn't show up today? What if I forgot what he looks like?"

Willie gazed down at me through narrowed eyes. "If he doesn't show this morning, we'll come back this evening. If he doesn't come today, we'll come back on Tuesday. And you don't believe for even one second that you won't recognize him, do you? He's your father, for cripe's sake!"

Arson stirred in the breast pocket of my school uniform.

"I think I'll know him." I said. But Willie couldn't understand how Father had begun fading away.

A security person whose grey and black badge blinked, "Lila A.," approached Willie and me. She pointed her scanner at our uniform pockets and even at our shoes.

"Why aren't you two in school?" Lila asked.

"We're on our way," I lied. "We have to meet our father here. He forgot something. We have to give it to him."

"You're brother and sister?"

"Sure." Willie backed me up. "Step-children, you know."

"Oh." Lila hardly seemed convinced. "All I've got to say is you'd better be out of here by 8:20, or I'll be reporting a couple of truants."

"Yes, Ma'am. 8:20 we've got it." I checked the time display on the commuter-rail wall. 8:13. Seven minutes.

76

I was too nervous to finish my chocolate. Willie drained the last drop from his cup and looked into mine.

"Aren't you going to drink that?" He asked.

"No, you have it." I handed Willie my cup, and he tilted it up. "Wonderful."

My eyes ached from scanning the crowd. Father had to come today; he simply *had* to.

"Why don't you tell me again what your father looks like?" Willie suggested.

"Oh, Willie, we've gone over it a thousand times."

"I know, but humor me."

"All right," I said. "He's tall, six feet six inches. His hair is blond, like mine, only now there are streaks of white at the sides and the top is thin."

"Yes, yes. I've got all that," Willie said, impatiently. "Tell me again about the walk."

"Well, he has this nervous habit. He taps his right thigh with his hand every other step. Like he's keeping syncopated time."

"Like that Rad-san maintenance person over there?" Willie pointed to a brown-uniformed, grizzle-bearded, bent shouldered person, with an official looking array of tools strapped around his waist.

The maintenance man was striding purposefully towards one of the half-dozen, free-standing hand cleansing units in the station. Every other step, his right hand patted his thigh.

"FATH..." I took a step toward him, but Willie jerked me back.

"Let go." I struggled against Willie's hold on my arm.

"Wait, maybe we should see what he does first. It might be dangerous to interrupt him."

"Are you crazy?" I could barely stand it. Father was less than fifteen feet away from me, and I couldn't even touch him.

"How many people did you say died in the accident?" It was more reminder than question.

"One hundred and forty-seven," I said.

"Let's not make it one hundred fifty by rushing things. Let's wait."

I thought I would cry. Then Arson began singing, and my racing heart calmed.

The song was different. This time, I could hear just as much as I wanted to hear, needed to hear, and remain anchored in reality at the same time.

"Ohhh," Willie murmured, before slipping into the normal dragon song trance. "Watch," he said, "wait."

19

Contact

Father set up a three-legged sign: *This Rad-san Cleansing Station temporarily closed.* Then he selected a tool and began dismantling the cleansing station.

I couldn't hear him over Arson and the rush of commuters as they headed for the embarkation portal, but I knew Father was probably humming while he worked.

I couldn't stand being so close to Father and not being able to hear his voice. I inched along the wall, away from Willie, toward Father.

A commuter-rail vehicle arrived. Workers who lived outside of District 5 and bleary eyed night workers disembarked. They pushed into the rail terminal. Some headed for the coffee dispensers, some walked straight to the doors on the opposite side of the terminal looking for the local connecting transit that would take them to the their work or their homes.

I was nearly close enough to speak to Father.

A woman, with straight black hair and olive colored skin, tripped over Father as he knelt before the Rad-san station. Father jumped up and helped the woman to her feet. I heard him ask, "Are you all right?"

"How clumsy of me," she said. Her voice, which should have sounded embarrassed or hurt, sounded tight and frightened. "Here you are working away, and I barrel right into you."

"No harm done," Father said. "Just let me brush off your knees for you."

Father bent over. With one hand he patted at the knees of her trousers, removing invisible dust. She bent, brushing her trouser legs too with one hand while the other hand slipped a small metal cylinder into Father's boot top.

"Thank you," the woman said. "Really, I'm quite all right now."

The woman started to move away. Father picked up the tool he'd dropped in the collision.

I took another step closer. Now, when Father raised his head I would be only a step or two away from him. I would be able to look into his face.

Arson's song stopped. Father raised his head. My father's hazel eyes looked confused. He didn't know me.

In all my *what-ifs* I had never imagined that I might have begun to fade for him, too.

Then his lips formed a silent question. "Cady?"

I took another step toward him. He motioned me to stop.

"If you need a hand-cleansing, young lady, you'll have to move along to the next station," Father said, turning away from me.

I opened my mouth to speak. From across the rail terminal there sounded a screeching voice.

"There she is! Don't let her get away!"

I looked up to see the black-haired woman turn on her heel for an instant, then bolt through the outer terminal door. Father watched, too. No one pursued the black-haired woman.

"Grab her! I tell you she's a subversive!" The shrill voice continued from the midst of a mob of Rail-security

80

people. The security people parted like a wave around a pier.

Nigel Quido led the charge.

20

Dragon Shadow

Willie was slowly coming out of his dragon-song trance. He was still too immersed in the other world to help me this time.

There was Father, standing close enough to touch, but with no clue what was going on around him.

I was in for it. No doubt about that. The important thing, the *only* thing was to save Arson.

Turning my back on the approaching wave of security people, I scooped Arson out of my pocket and thrust him into my father's hands.

"Take him!" I hissed between clenched teeth.

"But what...."

"He's a dragon. The only one in North America. Hide him! Save him!"

Then I turned around and strode towards Nigel Quido and the rail security guards. My hands were in the air like some hokey old west outlaw surrendering to a posse.

Mr. Quido grabbed me by the arm and shook me.

"Give it up young woman! Where is that slimy creature? Hand over the book."

"I don't have them anymore."

"Don't lie to me!" Mr. Quido growled. "Search her!" he commanded the security guards.

Lila A. scanned my body, head to toe with her instrument. "Nothing," she reported.

"You idiot! Of course that thing won't show anything. It isn't a bomb! It's a book! And a drag—err, chameleon!"

Quido knew! He was my knight in dented armor. He was my self-righteous Puritan.

An ice-like calm overtook me. I did not have Arson *or* the book. They could search me from now until the end of the world. They would find neither.

"Let me." Mr. Quido pushed Lila aside and roughly began feeling my body, starting at the shoulders.

"Keep your hands off her!" Willie shouted.

Mr. Quido jerked his head around. "Get that boy, too," he said. "He's in it with her!"

The guards were not so quick to move at the wild-eyed Quido's command, now. One did break away from the group and start toward Willie.

A shadow fell across Mr. Quido, and the whole room seemed to have darkened.

"Excuse me," I heard Father's voice behind me.

My heart sank to my stomach. Why didn't he just get away from here and take Arson with him?

Mr. Quido moved his hands down my arms, gripping so tightly he hurt me.

"I said, 'Excuse me,'" Father repeated, "But I don't think you should continue to touch her like that"

"Oh," Mr. Quido snarled, "Why is that?"

"Because, I don't like it," Father said.

"Humph!" Mr. Quido went on probing my arms.

"And neither does, *IT*," Father continued.

Mr. Quido and the rail guards looked up. Quido's fish belly face went even paler. His hands trembled on my arms, then dropped back to his sides.

There was a sound like the release of giant airbrakes, as people on every side of me gasped. All of the eyes that had been staring holes through me were now directed at high above and behind me.

I turned to see what was happening.

"Arson?" I could hardly squeak out the word.

He was gigantic! All of his colors were glowing brightly. The un-earned scales shone like ice. His lionesque head bent low as he hovered just above the terminal ceiling; his wing tips brushed the opposite walls of the terminal lobby. Smoke curled from his nostrils, as his shadow covered hundreds of people beneath him. Every one of those hundreds of people could see him for *exactly* what he was!

"Arson, you *did* it! They see you!" I felt tears stinging my eyes.

"Flap, flap'" Arson said.

The wind from his wings sent people whirling into chairs and walls, and onto the floor like fallen pieces on a chess board.

"Ummmm. Errrr." Nigel Quido said, when he righted himself again. "You see, I was right! This young woman has a dragon. Clearly against Illianamo ordinance."

"Uh huh," Lila said. "And what do you propose we *do* about that?"

"Well, arrest her. Take the dragon into custody."

"Sure enough, Mr. Quido. Why don't you wait here while I get the rope to lasso that thing. I'll let you have the honors."

"I hardly think that dragon corralling falls under the duties of librarianship."

"No? Well, I didn't sign on for it in my contract either," Lila said. "I tell you what we got ourselves here. We got us a clear case of shared hallucination. Like one of those visits from outer space that folks are always claiming to have. Don't you agree, Mr. Quido? And if anyone asks *us*, you're the head hallucinator. Isn't that right, guys?"

The other security people agreed.

"Now, young lady, since you've already missed the first period in school, why don't you see if you can't figure out how to get your over-sized friend out of here. And you," Lila pointed at Father, "help her out."

"Yes, ma'am," Father agreed.

Willie walked over to us. He extended his hand to Father, who, polite as ever, pretended not to notice the distinctive aroma surrounding Willie.

"I'm William Frederick Raimer," Willie said.

Father took Willie's hand, "Happy to meet you, William." Father glanced around nervously. But everyone was cutting us as wide a path as possible. It seemed whoever Father was hiding from was no exception.

When Father saw how people avoided us, he relaxed a bit. Father said, "Now, if any one has an idea how to get a fifty-foot dragon out of a three foot door, I'd be interested to hear it."

I was too exhausted to speak. I leaned against Father's side, and he dropped one arm protectively around my shoulders.

"Well, it's just a thought," Willie said, "But I have this theory on dragon size changeability, which, in light of certain recent occurrences, might have some validity. You see..."

Without thinking I opened the breast pocket of my school uniform. "Here you go, Arson," I said.

There was a flash of light and the smell of a sparking match. Suddenly, the space Arson had filled was dull and empty. I felt him warm and safe against my heart.

21

Explanations

Father escorted Willie and me onto the street. With his big hand gripping my elbow tenderly, he steered us through an alley way lined with "Rad-san" dumpsters. At the end of the alley was warehouse-like building with a danger-yellow sign attached to it. *"Posted—unfit for human habitation. Keep out,"* the sign warned us in a authoritative voice, as Father opened the warehouse door. We followed him inside.

In the center of the warehouse, beneath a glassed in panel of the roof, stood an impressive looking machine. On one wall there was a pile of blankets obviously slept in.

On top of the blankets rested a computer the size of Willie's—compact enough to fit in a generous-sized pocket. On the computer screen glowed a schematic for the machine.

I did not see any facilities for cooking, nor did I see a Rad-san station for cleansing. It seemed silly, but I wanted to ask Father how he had managed the everyday things if this was where he had lived for the past ten months. But Father beat me to the twenty questions game.

"You two took an awful chance today," Father said. "What if it had been a Rad-san enforcer yelling 'GET HER' instead of that crazy librarian?"

Neither Willie nor I could think of anything to say to that. Nigel Quido was the worst enemy I ever hoped to face. I couldn't imagine someone who would blow up an entire train to kill one man.

"How did you know where to find me?"

That question we were eminently prepared to answer, and answer we did. In detail.

We told Father everything: about Natalie Mondieu, about the plight of dragons, (specifically Arson), about the chart book for recording kind and brave deeds, and how it lead us to the commuter-rail station that very day.

"What I don't understand," I said, dumbfounded. "Is why Arson never changed sizes before."

"It seems perfectly obvious to me," Willie said.

"Oh? Please enlighten us."

"It's elementary logic, really. Tremendous size wouldn't have benefited us before. In the terminal, it was the only way to free his Charmer."

"Yes," Father agreed. "Not to mention your willingness to perform the ultimate act of courage and kindness. You would have sacrificed your life for Arson's. Perhaps in such extreme circumstances Arson has access to unusual amounts of reserve energy."

"Precisely," Willie said. "Like adrenaline in humans."

Then, as if that explained everything, Willie moved on. "Is this the machine for purifying water?" He pointed to the shining silver contraption in the middle of the warehouse floor.

"Yes. How did you know about it?"

"We deduced it. It was perfectly logical."

"Hmmm. Well, Marie Sun, delivered the final piece for my prototype today. I'd be willing to bet we'll find her name inscribed on quite a number of Arson's scales; along with Achmed Ali, Candace Roberts, and Eli Kingman," Father said. "They are the engineers who supplied me with the elements to construct it."

Willie hit his forehead with an open palm. "Of course if only Cady'd thought to track dragon-scales earned by other people which coincided with your deeds' dates and times, She could have tracked you weeks ago."

That was me all over—leading candidate for chump of the week.

"It was best she didn't. She might have given me away. Now, it doesn't matter," Father tapped his right thigh as he paced before his invention. "But it's better if I begin at the beginning."

"You see, I had the design ready to build the day of the commuter-rail crash. It's so simple, really, when I showed it to the other engineers they were all amazed. No one could imagine how it could *not* work."

"We were so confident, Eli brought in a bottle of wine after work and we celebrated in his office. Imagine how we felt when we heard about the rail crash. I remember Marie saying, 'Brian, you could have been on that train.' I'd bought my ticket just that morning."

As for me, I would never forget believing he *had* been on it.

"It was then that we began to suspect I might have been the target," Father continued. "When we checked my office computer, we found the plans for the system had been wiped out. Fortunately, I keep a copy of all my work on my portable." He pointed to the envelope-sized computer. "Of course, they were counting on that going up in the crash, too."

89

"And this is the 'Dulac system,'" Willie said.

"Yes, this is it. Of course the commercial model will be much larger, but even one this size can purify enough drinking water in an hour to supply District 5's needs for a whole week, with enough left over for a quick water shower besides." Father walked to the machine and inserted the piece Marie Sun had smuggled out for him.

"Some of us will *really* appreciate *that*," I said.

Willie gave me a garlicky look. "It's obviously solar powered," Willie said, "but how does it work?"

"Well," Father said, "it's a throw-back concept, based on a wedding of the old salt water distillation and multiple filtration methods...."

I stopped listening then, the blankets next to the wall began looking like a cloud designed for dreaming. I trudged over to them and sat down. There was only one thing I needed to know before I closed my eyes for the first time in what seemed like years.

"When are you coming home, Father?"

Father stopped explaining the machine to Willie. "I finish the prototype today. Marie and the others are bringing key members of the Environmental and Water Supply Boards here for a demonstration tomorrow. (Though the board members don't know that. They think they're getting a free lunch). I should be home by supper tomorrow evening. How does that sound?"

"Wonderful," I yawned. "I'll ask Mother to cook something besides potatoes."

Father laughed.

As I drifted off, it occurred to me that I hadn't changed Father's plans a bit. He would have been home tomorrow no matter what I had done. Unless, of course, there really

had been Rad-san enforcers in the terminal, and Arson had
scared them off with his sudden size-shifting trick.

I suppose I'll never know.

Epilogue

Christmas 2080 was the best ever.

Father was home. His machine was a huge success. And, all over the continent, Rad-san cleansing stations were being replaced by "DuLac Ablution Founts." (Willie thought up the name).

Now that Willie (and everyone else) can take water showers again, he has given up his garlic necklace. It hasn't made much difference in his popularity at school though. He doesn't seem to mind. He says, as long as he has one good friend, that's all he needs. Come to think of it, maybe that's enough for anyone.

Arson's size shifting exploits in the commuter-rail terminal more or less blew his cover—permanently. Some zoological experts came to examine Arson. They thought he'd make a great subject for display and study. They offered to build him his own habitat. We were *not* impressed. And since his *habitat* has always been the inside of a Dragon Charmer's pocket, there was really no way they could manage that and exhibit him, too.

Arson was declared a "Protected Species" by the Illianamo Tri-State Environmental Board. They named me his official protectoress. It seems a bit after-the-fact to me. But it made the government officials feel important, so that's okay.

Father has a standing order with the exotic foods company, for a case of kumquats and pomegranates every month. Now that we're the water purification barons of the planet, we can afford to eat exactly as we please. Potatoes have been banned from the DuLac dinner table until further notice.

Sara takes her after supper wishing trips on F. lap. Lately she's been wishing for a doll house con with functioning water showers.

Trash dumpsters are the only products the Rad- corporation is allowed to produce. That's the one use n replaced by Father's system. Rad-san corporation is unde investigation for the sabotage of the commuter-rail, but who knows how that will turn out?

I think about Natalie Mondieu a lot. I wonder if Arson ever size-shifted in her behalf. And how, if he did, she managed to keep him secret.

I wonder about other Dragon Charmers, too. Those in the past, those in the present, and those in the future. What dangers do they face? What sacrifices must they make in order to protect a rare and little understood species?

I wonder if I'll ever learn their names. No matter. It is enough to know that they exist.

Here's to Dragon Charmers everywhere: whoever they are, whenever they are.

Godspeed.